Mackabee and the Moonbeams

written by Laura Grenier & Bethany A. Marconi • illustrated by Marisa Bruno

To my loving family. –L.G.

To my three little men, Benett, Marshall, and Grayson. May your life be filled with amazing adventures! –B.A.M.

To my parents. –M.B.

To Mickey + Lizzy,
Reach for the Moon!
[illegible]

ISBN-13: 978-0615715681 (Bethany A. Marconi)
ISBN-10: 0615715680

The Moonie's, like all other moon families, were getting ready for their first night of the harvest season.

This was the first year that Mackabee was old enough to travel down the Moonbeams to Earth with his Mom, Dad, and sisters to collect wheat and corn. He was very excited!

At last, it was time to go. The Moonie's said goodbye to Crater the moon dog and headed out.

As soon as the sun dipped below the horizon, the glowing Moonbeams appeared. The Moonie's jumped onto the bright yellow Moonbeams and sailed down to Earth. Mackabee could not believe how many stars he saw as they whizzed by!

Finally, they arrived next to a large black rock surrounded by tall stalks of wheat. Mackabee, Bippy, and Pearly started to run off to play, but Mom and Dad stopped them. They reminded the moon kids that the Moonbeams can only be travelled on at night time so they had to be back to the black rock before sunrise! The children all nodded their heads and dashed away into the field while Mom and Dad gathered their crops.

The children flicked on their flashlight eyes and played cheerfully. Mackabee suggested that the wheat field was the perfect place to play Hide-and-Seek. Bippy and Pearly happily agreed.

After a few rounds, it was Mackabee's turn to count. He closed his eyes tightly and counted softly to himself.

When he got to ten, he popped open his eyes and searched for his sisters.

The field was a big place and there were so many great hiding spots. He looked under an old tractor and behind the haystack. Where could those girls be?

Mackabee stretched onto his tippy toes to look on top of an old barrel and noticed the night sky was not so dark anymore. In the distance, he heard his family calling his name. Mackabee began to run as fast as he could toward the large black rock.

When he finally made it to the meeting place, his family was already floating up the Moonbeams. Mackabee's father reached his arm down and Mackabee jumped as high as he could but he was too late!

As the moonbeams faded Mackabee began to cry. What would he do all alone in this strange place while he waited for the Moonbeams to return that night? Mackabee wandered through a field of green cornstalks until he stumbled upon an old barn. He opened the old wooden door and ventured inside. Tired and sad, Mackabee curled up on a pile of nice warm hay and fell asleep.

Mackabee was awakened suddenly by the sound of the barn door slamming shut. He hunched down behind the hay pile and peered around the corner. There in the doorway, he saw a small boy. He'd only seen them in pictures before so Mackabee was frozen with amazement at the sight of a real human!

Before Mackabee could sneak back behind the hay, the boy spotted him and screamed! Mackabee came out from his hiding spot and stood right in front of the Earthling and screamed back. Both boys began to laugh. Mackabee introduced himself and learned his new friend's name was Luke.

Since this was Mackabee's first day on Earth, Luke introduced him to life on the Blue Planet. He learned how to milk a cow, chase chickens, and swim in the pond.

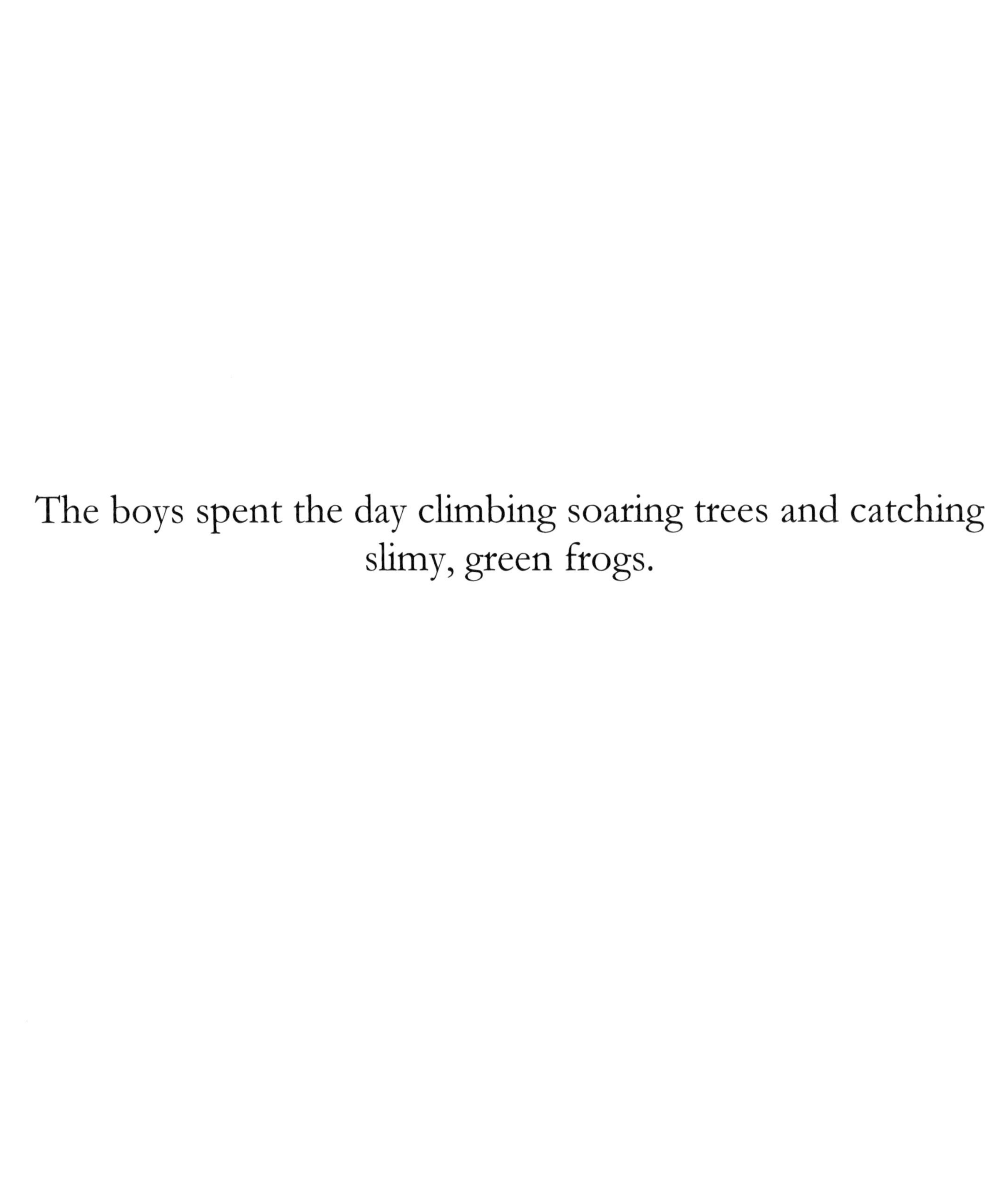

The boys spent the day climbing soaring trees and catching slimy, green frogs.

As the two new friends sat down to have a snack of chocolate chip cookies and fresh milk, Mackabee realized he missed his family. Soon the sun began to set and the boys decided to head back to the large black rock so Mackabee could go home.

They walked through the field and sat on the rock as they waited. As the sky darkened, the yellow Moonbeams returned and Mackabee spied Dad, Mom, Bippy, and Pearly floating down from the bright moon above. Luke and Mackabee hugged goodbye and promised to see each other again.

Luke snuck behind the rock and watched as his new friend stepped onto the Moonbeam and into the arms of his waiting family. Mackabee looked back over his shoulder and with a big smile, waved goodbye to his new friend.

The End

Mackabee's lost!
Earth Map
Start
Help Mackabee find his way back to his family in the field

Made in the USA
Charleston, SC
28 November 2012